# Snow White

First published in 2005 by
Franklin Watts
96 Leonard Street
London
EC2A 4XD

Franklin Watts Australia
45–51 Huntley Street
Alexandria
NSW 2015

Text © Anne Cassidy 2005
Illustration © Melanie Sharp 2005

A CIP catalogue record for this book is available
from the British Library.

ISBN 0 7496 6149 6 (hbk)
ISBN 0 7496 6161 5 (pbk)

**Series Editor:** Jackie Hamley
**Series Advisor:** Dr Barrie Wade
**Series Designer:** Peter Scoulding

Printed in China

# Snow White

Retold by Anne Cassidy

Illustrated by Melanie Sharp

## W
## FRANKLIN WATTS
### LONDON·SYDNEY

Once there was a beautiful but wicked Queen.

She hated her pretty stepdaughter, Snow White.

The Queen had a magic mirror. Every day she asked it:

"Mirror, mirror on the wall, Who is the fairest of them all?"

6

The mirror always
answered: "You, Queen."
But one day it answered:
"Snow White!"

The Queen was angry.
"KILL her!" she ordered
her huntsman.

But the kind huntsman
let Snow White go.

Snow White walked far into the woods. Suddenly, she found a house with small beds inside.

Snow White fell asleep. When she woke up, she found seven dwarfs there!

She told them about her
stepmother, the Queen.
"Stay with us!" they said.

Next day, the Queen asked her magic mirror:

"Mirror, mirror on the wall, Who is the fairest of them all?"

The mirror replied:
"Snow White!  She's living
in the woods!"

15

The Queen was even angrier. She made a plan to kill Snow White herself.

The Queen, dressed as an old lady, knocked at the dwarfs' cottage.

"Try these laces!" she said. The Queen pulled and pulled and pulled.

# Snow White couldn't breathe!

The dwarfs undid the laces and soon Snow White was well again.

Next day, the Queen came dressed as a pedlar.

"Here's a pretty comb," she said.

When the comb touched
Snow White's hair,
she fainted.

The dwarfs quickly took
the comb out.
"She's all right!" they said.

Then the Queen came dressed as a farmer's wife. "Share my apple," she said.

Snow White took a bite
and fell down as if dead.

The dwarfs were so sad.
They put Snow White in a
glass coffin.

Then a prince rode by.
He saw Snow White and
fell in love with her.

As he went to kiss her, the apple fell out of her mouth. Snow White woke up!

The Prince took Snow White to his castle.

They got married and lived happily ever after.

Leapfrog has been specially designed to fit the requirements of the **National Literacy Strategy**. It offers real books for beginning readers by top authors and illustrators.

There are 31 Leapfrog stories to choose from: